If Happy Ever Afters Did Exist

DeJane Penick

Published by DeJane Penick, 2022.

This is a work of fiction. Similarities to real people, places, or events are entirely coincidental.

IF HAPPY EVER AFTERS DID EXIST

First edition. August 11, 2022.

ISBN: 979-8215474761

Written by DeJane Penick.

Table of Contents

To my family and friends. Thank you for sticking by me and my dreams. I love you! :)

If Happy Ever Afters Did Exist

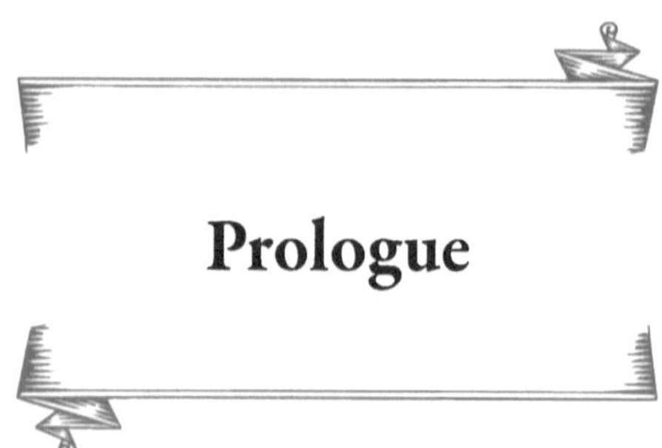

Prologue

Ever since I was little, I could see people's futures by touching them. When it first happened, I was frightened and started crying for my mom.

I told my parents and they thought it was just my imagination but then I predicted mom being pregnant with my little sister. That didn't happen until two weeks after. To test it out, they had me do it to all our family members and all of my predictions came true. When I touch them, I have a vision and see what happens.

It's mostly happy things, like my mom being pregnant, my uncle winning the lottery, etc. But rarely it's when it's bad things like how my aunt has cancer. I didn't realize I could see their deaths also until I touched my older sister, Sadie's hand.

It showed her in a dark room tied up with a tall man wearing all black. All of a sudden, he stabbed her repeatedly, making me scream. I told my parents and they immediately called the police and wouldn't let Sadie out of the house. I thought she would be mad but she was actually grateful. I mean why wouldn't she be? She could've died. But, I couldn't predict Sadie sneaking out. She was a teenager with a boyfriend that wanted to see her, of course, she would sneak out.

She didn't come back that night. Or the next night. Everyone and the police were searching all over the city for her. Her boyfriend, Hayden said that she never showed up for their date which made things worse.

One night, I was walking home and a van passed by me and drove to the pier. There was something off about it. For some reason, I decided to follow it. By the time I got there, they were parked beside the ocean.

Then, they threw something out. My heart dropped when I saw that it was a person. I ran towards the ocean, taking off my jacket while the van drove off. I should've paid attention to its license plate.

I dove into the water and saw the body. I swam towards it and my scream was muffled by the water. It was Sadie. Dead.

I carried her out and called the police with my hands shaking. The next hour was a blur. I barely remember anything. I only remember my parents talking to the paramedics while holding a sobbing Hayden in my arms while crying into his shoulder on the ground.

I always blamed myself for Sadie's death and I still do. If I had just tried harder to find out who that man was, maybe I could've saved her. If I had looked at the license plate, I could've told the police and they could've tracked them down.

I wish I hadn't seen her death in the first place. I hate this ability. What's the point of seeing the future if you can't change it?

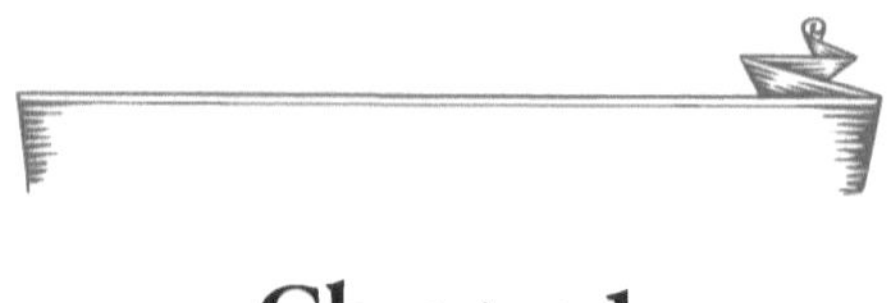

Chapter 1

I woke up to my alarm blaring. I yawned and turned over. I immediately smiled when I saw my boyfriend, Wyatt sleeping. We've been dating for three years now. I shut my alarm off and sat up rubbing my eyes. I stopped smiling when I realized what day it was. It's been seven years since Sadie died. I went to stand up but an arm stopped me.

"Don't leave," Wyatt mumbled.

"I have class, mumbles."

"Skip."

"It's college."

"Exactly."

"I'm already on his bad side because you made me late for five days."

"I'm lonely," he said, wrapping his arms around my waist.

I sighed while smiling.

"You're lucky I love you."

He chuckled as I leaned down and kissed him. Let's just say I was late to class again for "other" reasons.

After class, my professor gave me another warning and I left while texting Wyatt. He's definitely a bad influence on me.

Love <3

What did ur prof say?

If I'm late again, he's going to kick me out of his class

He doesn't have time for slackers

*But ur one of his top students *sad face**

I know but he says if I can't even come to class on time then how are you gonna handle the real world?

Don't worry, I have a plan

So do I

Ooo do tell

It's a surprise ☺

He was typing but stopped. Then, he typed again.

Do you need me to come with you today?

Don't worry I'll be fine

Are you sure?

Yes mother
Love you bunny ♥

Love you too puppy♥

I smiled and hurried onto the bus. I sighed as I looked out the window. Today is the day Sadie died. No one else in my family doesn't visit her grave. They said it was her fault for sneaking out. A small part of me agrees, but I just want my sister back.

After I visited her grave and cleaned off the leaves and overgrown vines, I went grocery shopping and went home to Wyatt and I's apartment. I smiled as our dog, Sammy, immediately ran to me. I smiled.

"Hi, Sammy."

I put the groceries on the table.

"Wyatt, I'm home!"

There was no answer. Then, Perfect by Ed Sheeran started playing. Wyatt went up to me smiling.

"What's going on," I asked, smiling.

"Ari, we've been dating for almost four years now, and they have been the happiest years of my life. Which is why I want to spend more with you."

He knelt on one knee making me cover my mouth while tearing up. He pulled out the ring.

"I love you. More than anyone in this entire world. Aries Ram Miller, will you marry me?"

I quickly nodded with tears running down my face.

"Yes! Definitely yes!"

I hugged him and he instantly hugged back. We kissed and he put the ring on my finger.

"I gotta call my uncle."

"Okay."

He started walking away. I grabbed his hand so I could kiss him again when suddenly I saw his future. I looked around and saw it was the alleyway that we always take to go home. It was so much darker now. Only one streetlight worked and it was flickering. I saw Wyatt walk past me with his earbuds in, holding a small bag. Suddenly, someone else walked past me. He was wearing his hood up and since it was dark I couldn't see his face. I was confused since barely anyone takes this way but then my heart dropped. He had an object in his hand. A knife.

"NO!"

I tried to jump in front but of course, he went through me. He stabbed Wyatt from behind making him stop and drop his phone. Before he could do anything, the hooded figure grabbed him by his hair and sliced his throat making me scream. No, no, NO! Wyatt fell to the ground. His eyes, which used to be full of life, stared right at me. Lifeless. Cold. I fell to my knees with tears streaming down my face.

"WYATT!"

Wake up. I covered my ears and closed my eyes. Come on, wake up, Aries. I opened my eyes and only saw Wyatt's lifeless body as the light went out. **WAKE UP!**

I opened my eyes gasping and saw Wyatt kneeling in front of me.

"Aries, what happened? You blacked out."

He's here. He's alive. For now.

Chapter 2

I didn't get any sleep last night. Or the next night. Or the next. Every time I close my eyes, all I see is Wyatt's lifeless body. His lifeless eyes stared right into my soul. Wyatt has been worried but after I stopped eating he became extremely worried.

I felt him shake me awake.

"Hey, Ari. You gotta get up, you know what your professor said."

"What's the point?"

"The point is you need a college education."

"You didn't go."

"On the contrary, I went to community college so haha. Plus, I love you but you need to shower."

I sadly smile. I'm gonna miss his humor. He turned serious.

"Are you okay? Ever since I proposed to you..."

My eyes widened. Shit.

"If you don't wanna get married-."

"I DO!"

He slightly smiled.

"Okay, save it for the altar."

"I'm sorry, it's definitely not you, just in a...writing slump. Yeah, my essay for class today is due."

"Your major is Psychology."

"You write essays in every major, Wyatt."

I got up and went into the bathroom. I undressed and got in the shower. I looked down and sighed as I let the hot water run down my face. Wyatt is going to die and I can't stop it. If these are my last days, weeks, or months with him then I should make them count. For him. I didn't notice I had started crying and wiped my eyes.

After I finished, I got out and wrapped a towel around my waist. I went back into our room and saw Wyatt watching Netflix. I gently grabbed his chin and kissed him. He kissed back and we pressed our foreheads together.

"I love you."

"I love you too."

I smiled and was about to get dressed when Wyatt.

"Don't get dressed in here. I'll lose my self-control. It's bad enough you're shirtless."

I laughed and grabbed my clothes. I went back into the bathroom and got dressed. I looked down and went back to our room.

"Are you planning on going anywhere?"

"Yeah, I'm picking my uncle up from the airport."

"Are you coming back here?"

"We'll probably go out to eat and then come back."

"Okay, just making sure."

He gave me a confused look but didn't question it. I went to class and was early for once. So early that the professor wasn't even there. I sighed and sat in front of the door. Soon after I fell asleep.

I woke up to the hallway being dark. How long was I asleep? I stood up and walked down the hallway. I turned the corner and saw Sadie. She walked away and I quickly followed her. She ran when she realized I was following her.

"Sadie, wait!"

I ran after her until the hallway came to an edge of a cliff. I went to grab her but she fell dragging me with her. We fell into the water and I screamed when I saw her body. She was covered in moss and her face was boney like a skeleton.

"You let me die, Aries," she sneered.

I tried to speak but the water kept getting into my lungs.

"And now you're letting Wyatt die too."

I looked over and saw Wyatt unconscious. Breathe. His throat was still slit. BREATHE! It's all my fault. **BREATHE!**

I swam to the surface and finally breathed in some air. I coughed off some water as I crawled onto land. I looked around and I was in the alleyway. I saw Wyatt on the ground and the hooded figure stabbing him repeatedly.

"Wyatt," I said weakly.

He stared right at me.

"Wake up."

I jumped awake at someone shaking me. I looked around panicking.

"Mr. Miller, it's me, Mitchell. You fell asleep."

I calmed down when I realized it was only a dream.

"Sorry," I said, wiping my eyes when I realized I was crying.

"Are you okay?"

"Me? Yeah, I'm fine, super fine. Anyway, I'm on time, I'm ready for class," I said standing up.

"It's a day off Mr. Miller."

"Huh?"

"Class is tomorrow, I just forgot some papers."

"Oh great, I got up early for nothing," I said annoyed.

I grabbed my bag and started heading towards the door.

"Mr. Miller."

I stopped in my tracks.

"If anything is going on, you know you can talk to me."

My grip on my bag tightened. I looked back and gave him a fake smile.

"I'm okay," I lied.

Chapter 3

I went into Subway to get my usual sub and waited in line. After it was finally my turn, my eyes widened when I realized who it was. Hayden. Sadie's ex-boyfriend.

"I didn't know you worked here."

"Well, now you do. Can I take your order?"

I frowned.

"Turkey Italiano."

"That'll be $4.25."

I gave him my money and waited for him to finish my sandwich. He looked up and saw the ring on my finger.

"When did that happen?"

"Three days ago."

"Congratulations. Someone found you attractive," Hayden said sarcastically.

"Thanks," I said annoyed.

He gave me my sandwich.

"It was nice talking to you, Hayden," I said sarcastically.

I headed to the door.

"I would've gone with you, I just…"

I turned back around.

"It's been seven years, Hayden."

"Don't you think I know that," he snapped.

His eyes soften.

"Sorry. I'm sorry."

"Hayden...when do you get off work?"

"Twelve."

"Do you wanna come over to my house?"

"Um...sure."

"Great, I'll wait," I said smiling.

I waited for his shift to be over. I texted Wyatt to see if he got home safe and he never responded. The more seconds went by the more I got anxious. Calm down, Aries, he died at night. But what if he died early? What if he got hit by a car instead? I saw Sadie get stabbed but she died by drowning technically.

"Aries," Hayden said, snapping me out of my thoughts.

I felt pain in my fingertips and they were bleeding. I didn't know I was biting them.

"Are you-?"

"We gotta go."

I grabbed his hand and ran out. After we got to my house, I ran inside.

"Wyatt!"

"In here!"

I sighed in relief. Hayden gave me a confused look.

"Well welcome to my lovely home."

"Yeah, it looks cozy."

Wyatt came into the living room and kissed me on my cheek.

"Who's this?"

"Wyatt, this is Hayden, my si-. My friend."

I almost said my sister's boyfriend.

"Hayden, this is Wyatt, my fiance."

"Nice to meet you," Wyatt said, holding out his hand.

Hayden shook it.

"You're very hot."

"Um, thanks."

"How'd you end up with this one?"

I punched him in the arm.

"As you can tell, Hayden is a dick."

"Language, Aries," Wyatt's uncle, Calum said, coming in.

"Oh, hey Calum. I forgot you were here."

"Wow, I'm deeply hurt," he said teasingly.

"Damn, he's tall," Hayden whispered to me.

I shushed him.

"Now that Aries is here...and a stranger. We should talk about the wedding."

"We're hiring someone," Wyatt said.

"We are?"

He shot me a look.

"I mean we are! We so are!"

"With what money?"

"Um, I hope you don't mind, my parent's inheritance money."

"Oh, of course, I don't mind, they left it in your name."

"But you have half."

"Well, anything for my nephew. When are you having the wedding?"

I looked at Wyatt.

"Aries answer," Calum said before Wyatt could say anything.

"Uh..."

I looked at Hayden and he shrugged. I looked back at Calum.

"Spring."

"Why Spring?"

"Well..."

Think Aries think. I thought about Sadie's birthday.

"Well my sister's birthday is in Spring and since she won't be here to see me marry my love, I want to do it on her birthday, so maybe she'll be there in spirit."

It wasn't completely a lie. I was hoping to ask Wyatt if we could have it on her birthday.

"That's sweet of you, Aries. When's her birthday?"

"Say May," Hayden mumbled.

I gave him a confused look.

"March 3rd."

"Oh good, we'll have the wedding in a week!"

Wait what? Wait, what day is it? I quickly pulled out my phone and it was February 24th. Damnit.

"Don't worry nephew, you don't have to lift a finger, I'll be back."

"Wait-."

He was already out the door. Wyatt sighed and stood up.

"Way to go, Aries," Hayden said.

"I didn't know what day it was!"

"I said say May, you say March of all months!"

"Because her birthday is in March, Hayden!"

"Okay, let's not argue. At least I get to marry you sooner," Wyatt said, smiling up at me.

"Yeah, that's good," I said sadly.

He gave me a quick kiss and went to follow his uncle. I frowned after he left and sat down.

"You okay?"

"I gotta tell you something."

"Okay," he said hesitantly.

"I saw Wyatt's future."

"That's never good."

"This guy...stabbed him from behind and slit his throat."

"Shit. Shit, Aries," Hayden said, starting to get up.

"Don't. He isn't dead yet but I don't know when he will be."

"Why don't you take a look again?"

"I can't. I can't look at that again."

"Do you wanna be surprised or know?"

I sighed as Wyatt came back.

"Well, his car is already gone."

I looked at Hayden. He did some sign language that I didn't understand.

I mouthed "I don't know what that means."

He mouthed back "I'll distract him."

I nodded and hesitantly grabbed Wyatt's hand while closing my eyes. I opened them and I was back in the alleyway. I saw Wyatt turn the corner. I ran up to him and looked as he turned on his phone. February 25th. Tomorrow? He dies tomorrow?

I saw the hooded figure come up. I quickly looked away and covered my ears as he stabbed him. I opened my eyes and I was back home.

"Wow, three years. I bet that little bastard didn't even invite me to the wedding."

"You bet right," I said, holding my head.

"Babe, are you okay? You were staring at the ceiling for a while."

"Yeah, just admiring our fine ceiling."

He gave me a confused look and sat next to me. I laid my head on his shoulder and sighed. Wyatt and Hayden got into another conversation but I blocked them out. I only have tomorrow left to spend with Wyatt. I'll have to make it count.

Chapter 4

"Babe? Baby," I said, shaking him awake.

"Hmm," he said, not opening his eyes.

"Brush your teeth I wanna play," I whispered in his ear.

He woke up to that and ran to the bathroom, making me laugh. I'm going to make this his best last day ever. After we fucked, we laid there out of breath.

"Not that I don't like doing what we did with you. Why did you wake me up at six in the morning?"

"I just want to spend the whole day with you."

"Well it's Saturday so can we spend the whole day at twelve?"

"Nope."

He sighed while smiling.

"You're gonna be the death of me."

I smiled and we kissed. After we got dressed, we went outside and walked around.

"Where are we going? Everything is closed."

"Just wait."

We went to the aquarium and I turned toward Wyatt.

"I need one of your Bobby pins Tarzan."

He rolled his eyes playfully and gave me one of his Bobby pins. I knelt down and picked the lock. I opened the door and held it for him.

"Wow, such a gentleman," he said sarcastically.

We laughed and went inside. Wyatt loves the water so why not let him see some ocean animals on his last day.

"Look at the sea turtles."

"Well, it is an aquarium."

"Thanks, smartass. Why did we break into an aquarium at six am?"

"Because it's always crowded and loud in here and we never got to see this."

I pointed up and Wyatt gasped.

"Woah," he said lying down.

I smiled and lay next to him. We stared at the sea in the ceiling. He reached out for my hand and I held it smiling. We stayed silent as we stared at the fish swimming.

"Can we just stay here forever?"

My heart broke and I started tearing up.

"I want to, I really want to."

"...are you okay?"

Before I could say anything, we heard a door slam. We both sat up and saw security.

"Hey! What are you doing in here?!"

"Run," we yelled in unison.

We got up and ran out the other doors while holding hands. We laughed as the security guard chased after us. Wyatt put his jacket down and jumped over the entry bar. I looked at him confused as I walked through the bar grabbing his jacket. I laughed as he rolled his eyes and held the door for me. After we left, we went to the beach and sat on the sand, watching the sea in silence, and listening to the waves.

"This is nice."

"Yeah."

"I love doing stuff like this with you."

"Me too."

Wyatt stared at me and I gave him a confused look.

"What?"

"You've been acting weird these past few hours. What's going on?"

"Nothing."

"Aries, we just broke into an aquarium and now we're at the beach. Are you breaking up with me?"

"No, of course not!"

"Then why have you been acting so weird since I proposed?!"

"I don't know," I yelled with my voice cracking.

I didn't even notice I started crying. I covered my eyes as I cried and Wyatt quickly put his arm around me.

"Hey, it's okay, we don't have to get married if you don't want to," he said softly.

"I want to, it's just…"

You're not gonna be here.

"Ari, look at me."

I looked up and he had tears in his eyes.

"I can wait, okay? I don't need a piece of paper to tell me that I'm gonna be with you forever. Married or not, I'm always going to be with you. No matter what."

That made me cry harder and he brought me closer. I'm gonna miss him so much.

After a while, we went back home. Wyatt said he was gonna buy some snacks real quick and I said okay. I got back home and took my jacket off. I sighed and sat down. Then, I thought of something. It was dark when he died. He was alone with a bag in his hand. It doesn't get light until seven. No. No, no, no. It's going to happen now. I started hyperventilating. No. I can't lose him. I got up and ran out the door. I can't let him die like my sister. I can't. I won't. I ran around the corner.

I saw him. Both of them. Wyatt looked up and smiled when he saw me. I ran to him as the guy got ready to stab him. Images of his death kept replaying in my head. That won't happen. I won't let it. I grabbed Wyatt's arm and turned him around so my back was facing the guy. I pulled him into a hug as the guy stabbed me from behind.

"A-Aries?"

The guy took the knife out and ran off as I fell to the ground. I heard Wyatt screaming at the guy as I held my wound. Suddenly, he was in my vision but he was blurry. I couldn't hear him but I smiled.

"You're alive," I whispered as I closed my eyes.

Chapter 5

I opened my eyes to a bright light. I looked over and saw Wyatt asleep. This must be Heaven. I looked on my other side and saw Hayden glaring at me. I guess not. I sat up and so did he.

"Do you have any idea what you have done?"

"Ari?"

I looked over and saw Wyatt waking up.

"Hey bunny."

He smiled and hugged me and I immediately hugged him back.

"You're finally awake. I thought you-."

I cupped his face in my hands and wiped away his tears.

"I'm not going anywhere."

"Um, Wyatt, you mind giving us some time alone?"

"Yeah, I'm gonna go get the doctor."

He gave me a quick kiss and left. Hayden smacked the back of my head.

"You idiot!"

"What? What did I do?!"

"You saved Wyatt! You changed the future!"

"I wasn't going to let my future husband die."

"Have you seen ANY time traveling movies?"

"I don't time travel, I just see into the future."

"Fine, have you heard of the butterfly effect?"

"Yes but enlighten me on what it is," I said sarcastically.

"Any small change can cause large, unpredictable effects."

"What's the worst that could happen?"

"Said every person in a horror movie ever."

"Look, I wasn't...I wasn't gonna let Wyatt die like I did with Sadie."

"And I get that but...you can't cheat death, Aries."

The door opened and Wyatt came in with the doctor.

"Hello, Mr. Miller. How are you feeling?"

"He got stabbed, how do you think he's feeling," Hayden said sarcastically.

I punched Hayden in the arm.

"I'm fine, just tired."

"Well thankfully, your attacker didn't do any serious damage but you'll have to stay here for three days. The police are here to ask some questions."

"Okay."

After an hour of trying to describe the guy and failing, the police left and Wyatt came in with snacks.

"I got your favorite."

He threw me a Twix bar.

"Thanks."

"So-."

"No more talking about the guy, please."

"I was going to say, can I have half?"

"Oh, yeah."

I broke it in half and gave it to him. We talked about random things for fifteen minutes before Wyatt stopped mid-sentence.

"Aries, your nose!"

"I know, it's big."

"No, it's bleeding!"

I felt underneath my nose confused. When I pulled my finger back, there was black blood on it. Before I could say anything, I started coughing up black blood. I could hear Wyatt calling for help but I couldn't breathe. My eyes rolled to the back of my head and all I saw was white.

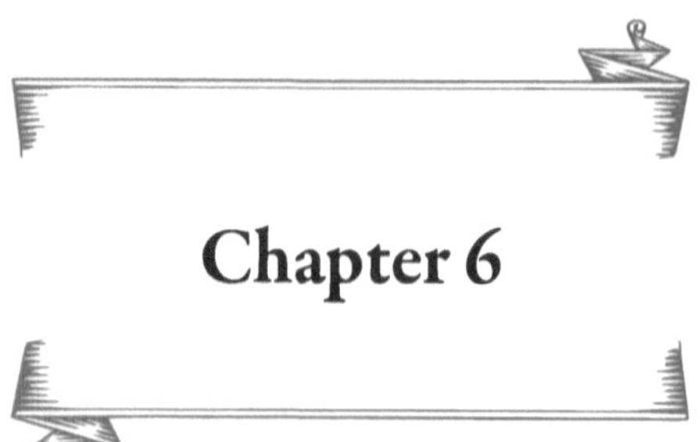

Chapter 6

I woke up in the hospital. I sat up and the room was empty.

"Wyatt?"

I got up and went into the hallway. I saw Wyatt talking to the doctors. After they walked away, Wyatt pulled out his phone to call someone. Suddenly, I heard creaking and so did Wyatt. We both looked up as the ceiling light fell on him.

"NO!"

I ran over to him and his head was split open. I screamed.

I woke up screaming. I sat up out of breath. I quickly got out of bed and ran into the hall. I saw Wyatt pulling out his phone. I looked up and saw the light swaying, about to fall.

"WYATT!"

He looked up as I tackled him. The light fell as we fell to the floor.

"Aries, you saved me. Again."

"Well, you could call me your knight in shining armor."

"But-."

"Are you boys okay? I told them to fix that light."

"We're fine," I said as we stood up.

I winced in pain as my wound started to burn.

"My wound hurts though."

"You probably reopened your stitches. Let's get you back to your room."

I followed him back to my room. I looked back at Wyatt and he had a perturbed look on his face. That was risky but he was about to die again. Why him? Why is the world trying to take him away?

I told Hayden what happened and of course, he flipped.

"I told you! Wyatt was supposed to die and now Death is trying to kill him."

"Shut up with the *Final Destination* shit! This was probably just a fluke."

It wasn't just a fluke. It kept happening again and again where Wyatt would get into situations where he would die and I ended up saving him. I got visions left and right which were now causing me pain both physically and emotionally. After a week, Wyatt, Hayden, and I were walking to the grocery store when Wyatt stopped to tie his shoe. That's when the safe above him decided it was the perfect time to fall. Hayden and I quickly found the rope and grabbed it right as it swayed above Wyatt.

"Okay, now this is getting ridiculous! How much bad luck can this guy have?"

"They're just-."

"Coincidences! I know! How many "coincidences" is it gonna take for you to realize that Wyatt needs to die?!"

Wyatt turned around at that. Well everyone did since Hayden yelled it. Wyatt noticed the safe above him and quickly crawled out from underneath.

"We're talking about a tv show," I said nervously.

Hayden and I let go of the rope after seeing Wyatt out from under it. Wyatt went up to us.

"Hey, I think we need to talk."

"Later, we'll catch up to you," I said smiling.

He gave me a sad smile and headed inside. I turned towards Hayden and he was looking down at something.

"Was the attack random or planned?"

"Random, you know the crime rates here are bad."

He picked something up and showed it to me. It was a bullet. I looked at him confused, still not getting what he was saying.

"Think about it. All the "coincidences", the near-death experiences. All of that happened because he wasn't stabbed right?"

"Right."

"Then, maybe, someone planned to murder him and you got in the way."

My eyes widened.

"So that means-."

"They still haven't finished the job."

Chapter 7

I put some snacks into the cart.

"We said we were going to eat healthier," Wyatt said smiling.

"And I said we shouldn't get a dog but look where we are now," I said, smiling back.

Wyatt smiled but it wasn't his usual smile.

"What's wrong?"

"Look, I may be stupid, but I'm not an idiot."

I gave him a confused look.

"I've been having a lot of near-death experiences and somehow...you always save me. How do you do it?"

I sighed.

"I guess you caught me."

I grabbed his hand and looked into his eyes deeply.

"I'm Spiderman."

"I hate you," he said as he started hitting me.

I laughed and pushed the cart.

"I'm being serious. This whole week, I could've died and you've saved me every single time."

"Wyatt, like I said, I don't know what to say. I guess I really do have a spidey sense."

He was about to say something but Hayden walked up with us with gogurts, Oreos, and gummy worms. I stopped him before he could put it in our cart.

"Put it back."

"But I'm craving it. Plus it helps me focus and I'm gonna need it when we-."

I kicked him in the leg causing him to yelp.

"Just put it in the cart."

He smiled and put it in the cart.

"I'll be in the car."

He left and we went to the counter.

"What's he talking about?"

"Well um, is there anyone you know that hates you?"

"No, I'm a sweetheart."

I snorted and he punched me in the arm while smiling. We started putting our stuff on the conveyor belt.

"Hey cutie, what's your name," the cashier asked.

"Um...Aries."

"How about you and I get together after I get off of work."

Wyatt laughed and I shushed him. I looked back at her.

"I'm sorry but I'm gay and engaged."

"Oh," she said in an annoyed tone.

There was an awkward silence as she started scanning our stuff. She threw our eggs into the cart.

"Look, you don't have to be rude."

"Well, I'm sorry that I'm not kind and gentle to faggots like you!"

I was taken aback by what she said.

"What the hell did you just call him," Wyatt said angrily.

"What? Are you his boyfriend?"

"His fiance you selfish, stuck up, b-."

"Wyatt!"

"$64.37. If you can afford it, you look like you can't."

"Oh we can, but can you afford to be jobless after what I do."

"Wyatt-."

"Do you know who my parents were? I own their company, I'll have you fired and blackballed for years so you can kiss your future goodbye.

Or you can accept my lovely fiancé's money and say "Have a nice day" with a smile."

They glared at each other. She snatched the money from me and forced a smile on her face.

"Have a nice day," she said through her teeth.

"Thank you."

We left and went to the car.

"You didn't have to do that."

"Yeah, I did. No one insults my fiancé except me."

I smiled while blushing.

"You called me fiancé twice."

"Well, you did tell her that you're engaged."

"Because I am."

He gave me a confused look.

"I wanna get married."

He smiled, got on his tiptoes, and kissed me. I kissed back and he pulled away. He pushed a stray hair out of my face.

"You're the most confusing person I've ever met."

"Only for you."

We were about to kiss again but Hayden started honking the horn.

"Come on! I wanna get home to my Oreos!"

We laughed and went to the car. Don't worry, Wyatt. I'm gonna find your murderer and they're gonna pay.

Chapter 8

"We should start on our guest list. You first."

"Well, obviously my uncle..."

If I take away the ones he's closest to, then maybe I can ask him about the people he hates. Then, we'll get somewhere. Maybe.

"And that's about it."

"What about any exes?"

"That would be pretty awkward."

"Well if you guys were on good terms then it wouldn't be. Unless there are some exes that are psychos. Are there? Is there?"

"...are you okay?"

"Yeah just making sure that there's not going to be any villain out there to ruin our wedding."

"Not that I know of."

If Wyatt has any enemies then I can make a suspect list.

"So, nobody hates you?"

"Well, there are a few people but I'm a pretty chill guy."

"Who are the few people?"

"Just people from High School. What is up with you?"

"Nothing, just curious about your past since we're getting married. Is that a crime?"

"Nope. Not at all."

Calum came in with a big book. He sat next to me and laid the book on the table and it made a loud thud.

"Oh my God," Wyatt mumbled.

"What's that?"

"It's the planner for your wedding day."

"And by your, he means his."

"I mean yours."

I opened the book and I smiled.

"Uncle Calum, no offense but we-."

"This is so pretty."

"Right? Don't the colors just pop!"

"It's beautiful. I've always wanted a big wedding like this. I always thought that I would never get the chance to."

I looked up and saw a flash of concern in Wyatt's eyes.

"Aww, do you hear that, Wyatt? Your lovely fiance wants a big wedding. It would be a shame if you ruined that."

I quickly remembered that Wyatt wanted a small wedding.

"We don't have to do the idea if you don't want to. Anything is fine with me, I just wanna marry you," I said smiling.

He smiled back at me and held my hand. He looked at Calum.

"Fine, we'll go with a Fairytale wedding."

"I knew you would come around. I'll go make some calls."

Calum stood up and went out into the hall.

"Hey, we don't have to. I know you don't want a big wedding."

"Like you said, you always thought you wouldn't get this kind of wedding. I want you to be happy."

I smiled and looked down. He gently put a hand under my chin and lifted my head up.

"Hey, we're going to get our Happy Ever After."

I really hope so.

Chapter 9

"His parents."

"His parents are dead, idiot."

"Then, his long-lost twin brother."

I sighed in frustration. Since Wyatt didn't tell me anything, Hayden is just calling out suspects.

"His uncle."

"Yeah, it's totally the guy paying for our wedding," I said sarcastically.

"Well, then I have nothing. This guy is the most mysterious bad boy I've ever seen."

Now that he said that out loud. Wyatt only told me that he was an orphan and he lived with his uncle since he was ten. He never told me about his past, his friends, etc. It was always about me. I'm so selfish! If I had just paid more attention to-. Paid attention.

"This is going to come out stalkerish, but what if we followed him for a day."

"Don't you have class?"

"I'll call in sick. I literally got stabbed, they'll take pity on me."

"Alright, but if we get arrested, I'll kill you myself."

The next morning, I pretended to be sick so Wyatt would think I'm in bed all day.

"Maybe I should stay home."

"NO!"

He gave me a confused look.

"I mean, I can take care of myself. I'm most likely going to binge-watch all the Twilight movies and make fun of them."

He laughed softly and kissed my forehead.

"Get better soon."

I waved bye to him as he left. I waited a few more seconds in case he forgot something and quickly got out of bed. I grabbed my jacket and crawled out the window. I climbed down the fire escape and ran to Hayden. He snickered when he saw me.

"Nice pajamas."

I was wearing unicorn pajamas since my other pajamas were in the wash. I shushed him and we watched Wyatt get in his car. He started the car and drove away. We quickly ran to Hayden's car and got in. Hayden started humming the Mission Impossible theme song and started the car. We drove after Wyatt.

"So where does Wyatt work?"

"At Starbucks."

He went silent and frowned.

"Isn't Starbucks the other way?"

He's right. Where's he going? We followed him for ten minutes and he led us to my school.

"What's he doing here?"

"Maybe he's having an affair with your teacher."

I glared at him and his smirk disappeared.

"Just a theory."

We got out of the car and followed him into the school. We peeked around the corner and saw Wyatt knocking on my professor's door.

"What is he doing," I asked.

Hayden shushed me.

"Don't shush me!"

Wyatt looked our way but we hid in time. Then, the door opened.

"May I help you?"

We peeked around the corner to watch.

"I'm Aries' fiance, Wyatt," Wyatt said, sticking out his hand.

Mitchell only glared at him, making Wyatt put his hand in his pocket.

"Look, it's my fault that Aries keeps missing class. Plus he got stabbed a few days ago because of me."

"Why are you telling me this?"

"Because the school will kick Aries out if he misses one more day and today is his last day."

"It is? I didn't know there were absences," I whispered.

"What I'm asking is, can you please tell them that Aries was here today?"

"I can't do that."

"Please. You and I both know that Aries deserves to be here."

"Wow, he really is a catch, I still don't know how you got him," Hayden whispered.

I punched him in the arm.

"Fine, just this once."

"Thank you."

"Of course and I better have an invitation to that wedding."

Wyatt smiled as Mitchell closed the door. Wyatt turned our way and we quickly hid.

"He's coming our way! Where do we go?!"

I looked around and saw the supply closet. I grabbed Hayden's hand and pulled him into the supply closet. Then, he started giggling, making me shush him.

"I guess you can say you're back in the closet."

I punched his shoulder as we heard a phone ring outside.

"Hello? I told you not to call me anymore Marco."

"Who's Marco?"

"I don't know, I can't hear because of your big mouth," I hissed.

"Fine, meet me at Starbucks in fifteen minutes."

We heard footsteps and then they were gone.

"Alright, he's gone, let's get out of here."

I tried to open the door but it was locked.

"Let me guess, the door's locked,"

"Yep."

"Nice hiding place, Ari."

"Just help me get the vent off."

Before we could, the janitor opened the door.

"How many times do I have to tell you people to stop making out in my supply closet?!"

"Sorry!"

We ran out and quickly fled down the stairs. We went to the parking lot and Hayden pulled out his keys.

"Man, which key is my-? Found it!"

"Hurry!"

"Okay bossy!"

Hayden unlocked the car and we got inside. Hayden sped to Starbucks and stopped the car hard making me hit the dashboard. I groaned in pain.

"This is why you wear your seatbelt."

I glared at him as we got out of the car. We put our masks on and went inside. We saw Wyatt sitting in a booth in the back by himself. He looked our way and we jumped inside the booth beside us.

"I don't think he saw us."

I peeked over the booth and saw him smiling making his dimples show.

"His dimples are so cute," I said gushing.

"Stop fanboying and get down."

I rolled my eyes and sat down. I heard the bell ding and looked up. A tall guy came in wearing sunglasses. He had tattoos on his neck and down his muscular arm. He looked at me and I quickly looked away. He kinda looks familiar. I looked back and he was still looking at me as he went over to Wyatt's booth. I guess I'm not the only one. The guy sat down at the booth.

"I wish we could hear them."

"Can I order my coffee while we're here?"

I noticed that the waitress was staring at us. I rolled my eyes and nodded. After a few minutes, the waitress came out with our coffees and we thanked her. I leaned back while pulling my mask off. I sighed and drank some of my coffee.

"*I told you I'm done.*"

I frowned and leaned closer.

"*You can't just be done.*"

"*Watch me.*"

I heard him scoff. I turned around and saw him looking at me sideways.

"*I think you should rethink your decisions. It would be a shame if I had to ask your lovely fiance.*"

Wyatt abruptly stood up, knocking their food and drinks off the table. Everyone looked over at them.

"Don't you dare bring Aries into this!"

"Well, I'm gonna have to."

Wyatt grabbed him by his collar and brought him over the table.

"If you even breathe near him, I'll-."

"You'll what? You won't do anything unless you want **him** to find out."

Him?

"If you guys are going to fight, take it outside, if you don't then I'm calling the cops."

The guy smirked as Wyatt let him go.

"Glad we could have this chat, Wyatt."

He stood up and left. Hayden sighed.

"Refill!"

"Hayden, I think-."

We jumped when we heard someone slam their hand on the table. We looked over and saw Wyatt.

"Hey babe," I said nervously.

"Did you hear all that? I don't know why you're following me but if you see that guy come near you, you run and find me and I'll handle it. Understand?"

"...yes," I said firmly.

He nodded and stood up straight.

"We'll talk at home."

He left.

"Well someone's sleeping on the couch tonight."

"That tattoo on the guy's neck. I saw the same one on the guy who stabbed me."

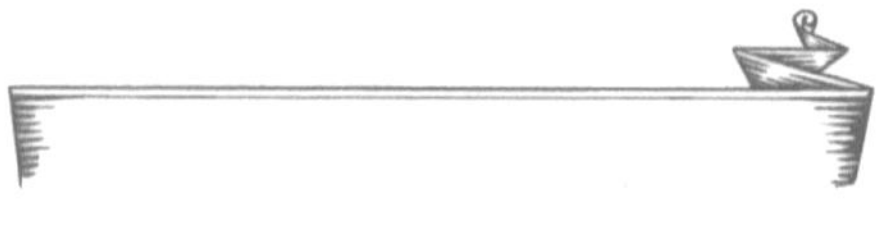

Chapter 10

"We have our murderer, case closed. Time to call the police."

"We can't, we don't have proof."

Hayden groaned.

"I hate all this Sherlock Holmes crap. Are there any cameras in the alleyway?"

"Only one but I don't know how we can get to it."

"Easy. We sneak in."

"Hayden, I don't know if you noticed, but we're taller than giraffes, how are we going to sneak in without being noticed."

"One of us will have to distract."

"Not it," I said before he could say anything.

"Why do I have to do it? It was my idea."

"Yeah but I'm younger and have more of a future."

Hayden groaned and headed toward the security guard.

"May I help you?"

Hayden punched him in the face and quickly ran away. The guard chased after him. I quickly went to the door and went inside. I went to the security footage of that night. There on camera was what happened. I was about to celebrate when I noticed something. Not to bring race into it but the guy Wyatt was talking to was black. The guy in the footage is white. They both have the same tattoo. I thought about what Wyatt said.

"I told you, I'm out."

Whatever these people are, they're in a gang and Wyatt was a part of it and he got out of it. Now they're after him. But if they want him back in, why would they murder him? Unless,someone went rogue.

"Stupid kid," I heard from outside.

I looked around for a way out and saw the vent. I quickly took the cover off and crawled through. After a while, I finally came to an exit. I turned around and kicked out the cover. I jumped down and landed on the hard ground. I groaned in pain and held my ankle.

"Best. Day. Ever," I said sarcastically.

I texted Hayden to call it a day and started walking home. I was brushing myself off when I bumped into someone.

"So-."

My eyes widened when I saw it was the guy from Starbucks.

"Well hello Aries," he said sneeringly.

I tried to go past him but he slammed me against the wall. I looked behind him and saw a guy recording us. My eyes widened. They're gonna send this to Wyatt.

"I think we need to have a chat."

"I'm actually in a hurry so if you could just-."

He grabbed my throat so I couldn't breathe. He lifted me up and I started hitting his arm but it was no use.

"Send this message to Wyatt. If he doesn't do this small favor for me, then Marco will just have to cut into your face."

He leaned in close to my ear so I could feel his hot breath.

"And I don't wanna ruin a pretty face like yours," he whispered in my ear.

He threw me to the ground and I gasped for air. I glared at him and flipped him off. He scoffed while smirking.

"Nice chatting with you, Aries."

They left and I laid there for a few minutes gasping for air. I'm guessing that's Marco. I stood up and leaned against the wall for support.

I limped home and went inside. Sammy immediately barked happily and ran to my feet. I smiled and petted him.

"Hey Sammy."

I limped over to the freezer and grabbed an ice pack. I sat down in one of the dining room chairs and laid the ice pack on my ankle. Then, all the events from this week started hitting me and I started sobbing silently. How am I going to save him when a whole gang is after him? This is so unfair. Why does the world always take away good people? Why did the world have to take Sadie? Why does the world have to take Wyatt away from me?

Suddenly, I felt arms wrap around me from behind. I melted into Wyatt's embrace and cried into the arms of his hoodie.

"I'm sorry, I'm so sorry," Wyatt whispered with his voice cracking.

"Please don't go. Whatever it is, don't go."

"...I won't. I promise."

Chapter 11

Later that night, I couldn't fall asleep. Because I knew he lied straight to my face. I heard him sit up and I immediately wrapped my arms around his waist. He sighed and gently unhooked my arms. He went out into the hallway.

"Hey, where do you wanna meet? Alright, I'll be there in twenty minutes just...keep Aries out of this."

I heard him sigh and come back inside. I kept my eyes closed as he got dressed. There was silence for a few moments before I felt him kiss my forehead.

"I love you."

I heard him leave and opened my eyes. I quickly got out of bed and put on my jacket. I waited a few more minutes before leaving. I went down the alleyway quickly. I turned the corner and screeched when I saw Wyatt standing there waiting for me.

"I knew it."

"Wyatt, you can't do this."

"I'm doing this to protect you."

"I can protect myself."

"Not against these guys. Go home."

He was about to walk away but I walked in front of him making him stop.

"Not until you tell me what your deal is with these people."

"No."

He was about to walk around me but I put him against the wall.

"Wyatt, I'm not losing you too!"

We both went silent. I realized what I said and backed away.

"Sorry."

He sighed and ran a hand down his face.

"Look, you're not gonna lose me. I promise."

"You can't promise that."

"...I know."

We laid our foreheads against each other.

"Ari I-."

Suddenly, I felt hands grab me from behind and throw me to the ground.

"NO!"

I looked up and saw someone holding Wyatt back. I looked up and saw Marco.

"Hey sweetheart. Miss me?"

"Not even a little bit."

He chuckled and kicked me where my stab wound was making me shout in pain.

"Get away from him, Marco! This is between you and me!"

He ignored him and circled around me. He knelt down next to me.

"You know it's okay to be scared. A lot of people are scared of me."

"Why? Because of your face," I spat out.

He chuckled. He grabbed me by my hair and slammed my head down hard onto the pavement making me groan in pain.

"Your fiance is funny, Wyatt."

Dark spots had clouded my vision and there was ringing in my ears. I felt him slap me.

"Hey, stay with us, Ari. We're not done yet."

I sat up to see him raise a bat with nails in it under my chin.

"This is Batanail. Heh, get it. Because it's a bat with nails in it."

"Marco don't!"

Marco got up and punched Wyatt in the nose. I was about to get up but one of the guys blocked my way. How many are there? Marco grabbed Wyatt by his chin and forced him to look at me.

"You see him? Now I want that pretty face to stay on him so for that to happen, you need to shut up," Marco growled out.

Wyatt didn't say anything but he was breathing heavily. I could tell he was full of anger. Marco went back over to me and patted my head. He stopped in his tracks and ran his fingers through my hair.

"Your hair is so soft. What shampoo do you use?"

I glared at him. Marco only smiled and looked up at one of the guys. They nodded and punched Wyatt in the stomach, making me clench my fingers. I need them to keep their focus on me.

"I don't use any."

"Wow, wish my hair was like that."

He circled around me again while dragging his bat on the ground.

"So, we have a problem. See your fiance here owes us something but it looks like he can't provide that so."

He stopped in front of me and got close to my face.

"I'll just have you instead."

Everything was muffled after he said that. Wyatt and I are gonna die here if I don't think of something fast. I looked at Wyatt and he was begging with tears streaming down his face. I looked back at Marco who had a sinister grin on his face. That's when I thought of an idea.

"I have a better deal."

"And what's that?"

"If I can predict what's going to happen to you in the next 60 seconds, then you have to let us go."

He snickered.

"What are you? A psychic?"

"You could say that."

He laughed, making the others laugh.

"Fine, predict my future."

I have to focus. I can't go too far. I grabbed his wrist tightly and I gasped for air. It hurts. **IT HURTS!** His future flashed by quickly. I looked up to the lamp post and it exploded and fell on top of Marco. I came back to reality and Marco was frowning. His smirk was gone. Any playfulness disappeared. I heard static and creaking as my nose bled.

"Move."

Marco looked at me confused before he looked at the lamp post.

"Shit!"

He moved out of the way in time as the lamp post fell. It smashed to pieces causing it to catch on fire. I tried to get up but the world started spinning. Wyatt. Where's Wyatt? I felt someone turn me around and I tried to get out of their grip.

"Ari, it's me, we gotta go."

He turned around so I could get on his back. I got on and he immediately stood up and started running. Everything was turning black.

"Wyatt," I whispered.

"Stay with me, Ari!"

I can't. I'm sorry. Everything went black.

Chapter 12

I woke up to darkness. I sat up and I was in my old room.

"Wyatt?"

I got out of bed and went into the hallway. I heard someone humming and went towards it. It led me to the kitchen and I saw my mom.

"Mom?"

She ignored me. I tried to tap on her shoulder but my hand went through. Is this a vision? Suddenly, I felt someone go through me. It was my dad. He hugged my mom from behind. They started making out and I looked away in disgust. I went to my little sister, Lily's room and saw her on her phone.

"Lily?"

She turned towards me and her eyes were gone. I backed away as she stood up. My back hit the hallway wall and I went back to the kitchen. But then, I saw a bunch of men in cloaks. My mom and dad were on fire and screaming in agony. I started hyperventilating as they came toward me. I ran to my old room and locked the door. I blocked with my dresser and backed away out of breath. Then, someone threw me onto the bed. I looked up and saw Sadie on top of me. She wrapped her hands around my neck and started burning me. I screamed in pain.

I screamed while holding my throat. I opened my eyes as tears ran down my face. I stared at the ceiling trying to catch my breath. Wyatt ran in and quickly got into bed as I sat up, shaking.

"Hey, what happened?"

"N-Nothing."

"Ari-."

"I'm fine, I just need a minute."

He nodded and got up as I held my chest. I turned to look at him and he was playing with his fingers.

"Are you okay?"

"Are YOU okay?"

"It was just a nightmare."

"I'm talking about what happened with Marco."

I forgot he saw that. Should I lie? But he was going to find out sooner or later.

"I can see into the future."

"Like a fortune-teller?"

"Yeah kinda. I've been able to do it since I was five. I just touch people and see their futures. Like if you won the lottery or...if you die."

"...Did you see my death?"

I bit my lip and nodded.

"So, you've been seeing my deaths this whole time? That's how you've been saving me?"

"I'm not supposed to. I'm supposed to just let it happen but I couldn't. Not with you."

He looked down and I looked at him confused.

"Why are you even believing me?"

"Because it makes sense. Plus, you've never lied to me before."

We stayed silent for a few moments.

"What happened after I passed out?"

"I took you to my uncle's apartment."

That's when I noticed that this wasn't our room.

"Are they going to be after us?"

"...probably."

I sighed.

"One of them murdered you. Someone white with black hair."

"They wouldn't murder me since I owe them something."

"That's what I said. So one of them must have a grudge against you. What do you owe them?"

"...I can't tell you."

"I just told you my past."

"Well I'm sorry but I can't tell you."

I sighed.

"Look, if we're going to find your murderer, then you need to trust me."

"I do trust you, I just...can't."

"Wyatt-."

"Ari, I appreciate you trying to save me but...sometimes you just can't save people."

I glared and took his hand. I gasped in pain as his skin burned me causing me to pull away.

"What the hell?"

"I told you. You can't save me. It's hurting you that I'm alive."

"Wyatt, you should know by now that I'm not giving up on you. So like it or not, I'm saving you and we're going to have a beautiful fairy tale wedding and adopt three kids."

"Two."

"Three."

"I do not want three kids. This isn't Full House."

"Three," I said firmly.

"Fine but they better be girls."

He chuckled.

"We're not even married yet and we're talking about kids."

I smiled and looked down.

"Ari?"

I looked up and his smile was gone.

"If I tell you my past. Promise me you won't freak out."

"I'm not going to freak out."

"...trust me. You will."

Chapter 13

5 years ago

I woke up to someone slamming their hand on my desk.

"Mr. Franklin, if you're only here to sleep then maybe college isn't right for you."

"I'm awake. I promise."

He rolled his eyes and went back to the front of the class. I sighed and ran my fingers through my long hair.

I had to work two jobs to keep my apartment. I didn't want to be a burden to my parents so I never asked them for money. Every time they called, I just pretended that everything was fine.

"Hey, I heard you had problems staying awake," the guy next to me whispered.

"I don't want to buy any drugs," I said while doodling on my paper.

"Then, how about I solve your money problems?"

I dropped my pencil and looked at him confused.

"How did you-?"

"I have my ways. I'm Marco."

"Wyatt."

"So, recently my job has taken a hit of employees and now we're short. So, we're looking for help. It pays well so you can quit both your jobs."

"What's the job?"

He smiled.

"Selling brownies."

I scoffed.

"No thanks."

I went back to drawing and thought that was the end of the conversation.

"It pays a thousand dollars per week."

I dropped my pencil again.

I should've said no but I couldn't.

I turned towards him and he had his hand out. I hesitantly shook his hand.

Back then, I didn't realize that I had just shaken hands with the devil. After a week, I was one of their top sellers. But the job was even more exhausting than my last two jobs. So, I saw that one of the drugs was Adderall and took some. The client was obviously mad that some of his product was missing but Marco swore to him that it was all there and if he had a problem then buy somewhere else. So, for the next two weeks, I started taking some products out and keeping them for myself. I didn't get caught until one of the coworkers was pissed. He started blaming me and said that I stole from him. I kept denying that I didn't and Marco said he believed me. I shouldn't have believed him. The night before, I got a call from one of my old friends, and...my parents' house was on fire. I ran as fast as I could but I was too late. The house was engulfed in flames and my parents were dead. Marco was there and he whispered in my ear.

"Never steal from us again."

After that, I wanted out but Marco said that I was already too deep. If I left now, then I would have to pay back every single paycheck they gave me. I told them I would and I've been paying them back ever since. I gave them the last of it and I thought that was the last of it. But Marco says I still owe them the drugs I stole and I couldn't get them that. So they want me to rejoin them but I always decline. They couldn't force me because they had nothing on me. Until I met you.

"I don't know how they found out we were getting married but now you're in danger and it's my fault. I don't want you to end up dead like my parents. I can't let that happen to you too."

He looked down while biting his nails to keep tears from coming out. I gently took his hand and he looked at me confused.

"I told you, Wyatt. I'm all in. I'll always be with you."

He sighed.

"And that's the problem. Aries, I love you, but until they go away..."

My heart shattered into pieces when I realized what he was trying to say.

"No."

"We have to."

"No, we don't. We'll find a way!"

"There is no way, Aries! As long as we're together, they're going to keep coming after you and I can't let that happen. I can't let you ruin your life for me!"

"I don't care!"

He scoffed.

"See, that's your problem, Aries. You never think about yourself. You may not care if you die or not but the people who love you will. Your little sister, your parents, even though he won't admit it but Hayden too, and mostly me. I will go out of my mind if you die because if you do, I feel like that's on me."

I was going to say something but stopped myself. He's right. I let out a shaky breath and nodded. He grabbed the sides of my face and kissed me and I kissed back while crying. He pulled away and I saw tears streaming down his face.

"I love you," he choked out.

I smiled and wiped his tears away. I have to be strong for him.

"I love you too."

I stood up and grabbed my jacket. I went to the door and reached for the knob. Don't look back. If I look back, I won't be able to leave. I opened the door and left while closing it behind me. I slowly went down the hallway and stopped at the stairs. That's when I broke down into tears and slid down the wall. I could hear nothing but my sobs echoing throughout the hallway and my heart breaking.

Chapter 14

"We're still helping him?!"

"Yes."

"Have you finally lost your MIND?!"

The night after...the incident, I went to Hayden's house and told him everything. I also told him that Wyatt's murderer was one of them.

"Whether Wyatt and I are broken up or not I'm not letting him die."

"Do you even know when his next death will be?"

"I tried but his skin burned me."

"That's because you've saved him fifty times! Aries, just let him-."

"Put yourself in my shoes."

"What?"

"If you had my power and you saw Sadie die right in front of you. Wouldn't you do everything you could to prevent it?"

"Of course, I would," he said with no hesitation.

"Then, you understand why I'm doing this."

"...yeah."

"Good, now here's what we know. The guy that stabbed me was white."

"Great, that rules out half. What about the other half?"

"That's what we gotta find out. Wyatt said that one coworker was so pissed at him. What if that same coworker was the one that killed him?"

"How do we find that out?"

"Well, we can't ask Wyatt so the only way is to see for ourselves."

His eyes widened.

"No. No. NO!"

"They don't know who you are. When Marco was staring at me, he was staring at **only** me because you had to tie your shoes."

"You're trying to kill me, that's what this is. Quick, look at my future."

I rolled my eyes and touched his arm only for it to burn me.

"I guess I can't look at anyone's future right now."

"I'm gonna die."

"You're not gonna die, we just have to do this carefully so nothing goes wrong."

"What's your plan?"

"Alright, so Marco is looking for recruits. You just have to go up to him, ask him if you can join, get friendly and ask about what happened between the guy and Wyatt."

"That seems complicated."

"Just trust me."

"How do I even know where to find him?"

"I don't know, go to the sketchy parts of town."

"Where will you be?"

"School so I don't get kicked out."

"Can't we send Lilly?"

"Hayden!"

"Fine, we'll just risk my precious life," he said, leaving.

Like it was ever precious. I got ready and headed off to class. While in class, I could feel Mitchell's eyes burning a hole into my forehead the whole time.

"Class dismissed. Mr. Miller, I would like to have a word with you."

I gulped. I went down to him as everyone left.

"I heard you got stabbed a few days ago. Are you feeling any better?"

"Oh, yeah, it still hurts sometimes but I'll live."

"Well I'm glad you showed up to class but we need to talk about your grades."

Oh great.

"I'll pull them up for you."

He went to his computer and the right side of his jacket fell off his shoulder. My heart dropped when I saw the tattoo on his neck.

"Why are you telling me this?"

We already know each other. That's what he was trying to say. Wyatt introduced himself because he knew we were following him. He glared at him when he tried to shake his hand. He knows where we live. He knew we were getting married. It's him. He murdered Wyatt.

Chapter 15

Hayden. I gotta call Hayden.

"Um, Mr..."

Man, what's his last name?

"Do you seriously not know my last name? You've been here for almost a month."

"Yeah but I always call you Mitchell. Look, I just remembered that I had an appointment with the dean to discuss my grades," I lied.

"Oh well go ahead."

I quickly grabbed my bag and ran out. I pulled out my phone as I ran to my car. I called Hayden as I got in.

"What now?"

"It's Mitchell!"

"Who's Mitchell?"

"My professor. He's the one that murdered Wyatt!"

"What?!"

I was about to say something but then I heard my car door open. I turned around as Mitchell covered my mouth with a rag. I tried to get out of his grip but he was too strong. Soon enough, I started seeing dark spots and everything was black.

I opened my eyes to everything blurry.

"Well, look who's back."

I tried to see who was talking but it was too blurry.

"Who are you?"

"Aw, he doesn't remember me. How about I remind you."

They grabbed me by my collar and made me look at them. Fuck.

"Marco," I growled out.

"Hallelujah, he remembers! Now we can begin."

"Why are you whispering?"

Everyone started laughing, making my head hurt. I tried to stand up but I only fell back down. I can barely feel my legs. I tried to move forward but my hands were chained behind me.

"Hey Wyatt, look who we have. Now if you want your lovely fiance back, you'll rejoin us, if you don't then..."

He grabbed my hair roughly to make me look at the camera.

"Then I'll just have to hurt this pretty face more than I have to."

Suddenly, he slammed my head to the floor causing a loud ringing to echo through my head. I screamed in agony as I lay on the floor.

"Damn, my bad, Ari, didn't mean to do that hard."

"Help me. Someone help me," I whispered while sobbing.

"Aw, poor baby."

He grabbed me by the back of my neck and kissed me. I tried to pull away but his grip on my neck was too strong. He pulled away and I gasped for air.

"Been wanting to do that for a while."

Then, one of the guys in the room went to me and put a needle in my arm making me inhale sharply.

"Good night Ari."

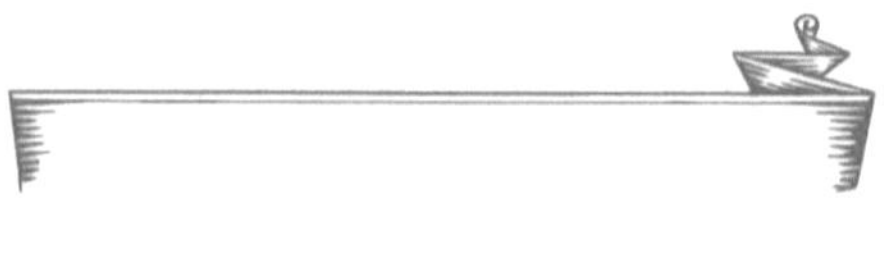

Chapter 16

I woke up to someone shaking me. I quickly backed away, panicking.

"Ari, it's just me.," Wyatt said.

"Wyatt...your plan didn't work."

"I know, I'm so sorry, Ari."

"Oh, I'm glad it didn't work because one, I can say I told you so and two, we get to stay together."

"Ari-."

"Wyatt, like you said, "We're going to get our happily ever after."

He smiled and he grabbed the back of my neck and we kissed. Now that's more like it. We heard a door slam and pulled apart. Wyatt barely turned around before he was knocked out by Mitchell.

"And to think I asked for an invitation to your wedding. Now I won't even get to go."

"Why are you murdering him?"

"Because I was the best seller here until Wyatt came along. He was getting paid more even though we kept losing clients because of him. Then, I found out he was stealing the whole time, and guess what? No one believed me and they fired me. My life was ruined by some snot-nose kid. When I found out his parents were killed, I wasn't satisfied. The only way for me to be satisfied was to watch him take his last breath. I was a professor for years, wondering if he was going to come back. I was going to give up, but one day, I saw one of my students holding hands with him, which was you."

I brought Mitchell right to him.

"But there's still one more thing that makes me curious. How did you know I was going to murder him?"

I glared at him, making him sigh.

"Of course, you're not going to tell me. Your sister was the same way."

Wait, what?

"How do you know my sister?"

He had a sinister smile on his face.

"Just following the boss's order and the boss said he would take me back if I murdered Wyatt so."

He pulled out his gun. I tried to stop him but I was still chained to the wall as Wyatt was coming to.

"Now, I get to start anew with the boss."

He started giggling.

"Looks like this is where your fairy tale ends."

Then he was knocked to the ground and out cold. I looked up to see Hayden holding a bat.

"Mitchell forgot about one thing about Fairy Tales."

Hayden knelt beside Mitchell.

"The heroes always win."

"You just wanted to say something witty huh?"

"Absolutely."

I heard Wyatt groan and I tried to make my way to him but got held back by the chains.

"You didn't happen to pick up a key by any chance did you?"

We heard police sirens coming our way.

"No, but I'm guessing the police do."

After the police helped us and arrested all the gang members, we had to go to the station and give statements for four hours. We finally went home and I face-planted onto the couch. Of course, Sammy immediately ran to us.

"Home sweet home."

Wyatt laid on top of my back making me pretend to groan and making him hit me. But I could tell he was smiling.

"So, can we finally have our wedding without the both of us breaking up with each other?"

"Absolutely."

That's all I ever wanted.

Chapter 17

Our wedding was beautiful but of course, I'm biased. Hayden was my best man and Lily was Wyatt's best woman since he's close with my family. My parents didn't show up, I wasn't expecting them to. Ever since Sadie's death, they always blamed me for it. But a part of me was hoping they would show up for their own son's wedding.

"I'm the only thing close to a bride so here we go ladies," Lily said.

She threw the bouquet and all the ladies lunged at it, making me laugh. I felt someone sit next to me. I looked over and saw Hayden.

"The wedding turned out how I thought it would be. Cheesy," Hayden said.

"Even on my wedding day, you're a dick."

"Yeah well, I'm the closest thing to a big brother that you have."

We laughed and we went silent. I started playing with my fingers.

"I wish Sadie was here."

"...Sadie would've loved this. Cheesiness runs in the family."

I laughed and he chuckled. Then, Perfect by Ed Sheeran started playing and I saw Wyatt on the dance floor.

"Looks like I have to dance."

"Just like the end of a Disney movie."

I laughed and stood up. I made my way through the crowd to Wyatt. He looked beautiful under the light. His hair was up in a bun and he was smiling, showing off his cute dimples. I stood in front of him.

"May I have this dance," I asked.

"Why yes my love," Wyatt said smiling.

He put his arms around my waist.

"Since I'm taller, aren't my arms supposed to go on your waist?"

"Just put your arms around my neck, giraffe."

I smiled and put my arms around his neck. We swayed to the music.

"I'm glad we got our happily ever after."

I smiled into his neck and closed my eyes.

"Me too."

We finally got our happily ever after. I opened my eyes and frowned. But something doesn't feel right.

"Hey, you okay? You just got tense."

"Yeah, just...overthinking."

I lifted my head off his shoulder and my eyes widened. There was blood on his neck. I felt underneath my nose and it was bleeding.

"Babe?"

I pulled away while holding my nose.

"I-I'm fine, I'll be right back."

I quickly left the ballroom and ran to the bathroom. Everything started spinning and everything was blurry. No, no, no. Not now! I looked in the mirror and my nose was pouring down blood. I got some paper towels and held them to my nose. I heard a knock on the door.

"I'm okay, Wyatt," I lied.

"It's not Wyatt."

"Who is it?"

"The person who paid for all this."

I sighed and sat on the counter while holding my head. He came in like I knew he would.

"Are you okay?"

"Yeah, just a small nosebleed."

He noticed the blood on the floor and all the bloody paper towels.

"Yeah, I don't think small is the case here."

"I just get nosebleeds sometimes. I'm okay."

"Well if you need anything, just know I'm here for you."

"I appreciate it and thank you again for paying for our wedding."

"Of course. I would do anything for Wyatt. He's like a son to me and now you are too."

I smiled as he left. I pulled away the paper towels and looked in the mirror. My nose had stopped bleeding and I sighed in relief. Hopefully, that was the last of this.

Chapter 18

It wasn't. Since that day, it was like I was getting sicker and sicker. We couldn't go on our honeymoon because I wouldn't stop throwing up every five seconds. Wyatt took days off of work but we still had bills to pay so I told him I was fine. I also got a call from my school and I was officially kicked out. On the bright side, at least I have more time on my hands.

I washed my hands after using the bathroom and looked in the mirror. I quickly looked back down when I saw a figure behind me. I haven't been sleeping that much either so I've been hallucinating. I washed my face with cold water and let out a shaky breath. I hesitantly looked up and the figure was gone. Wyatt was at work so I was home alone. I sighed and opened the door only to slam it shut. The figure was out there. I backed up to the wall as I heard it pound on the door.

"It's not real. It's not real. It's not real," I repeated while covering my ears and closing my eyes.

I slid down the wall and waited. I fell asleep against the wall and woke up to the front door closing. I started hyperventilating but calmed down when I heard Sammy run through the halls and Wyatt's voice. I grabbed the counter to lift myself up. I looked in the mirror and was confused. The bags under my eyes were gone and I was no longer pale. I felt better than I had been in weeks. I opened the bathroom door and went to the living room. I saw Wyatt petting Sammy.

"Hey."

"Hey. Are you feeling better?"

"Yeah."

"Good, because I was going to take Sammy for a walk. Wanna come with?"

"Sure, I need some air."

Wyatt put Sammy's leash on him and we walked through the park while holding hands. I noticed my shoe was untied and let go of Wyatt's hand.

"My shoe is untied, I'll catch up."

He nodded and went ahead with Sammy. I knelt down and tied my shoe only for it to start raining. I sighed as I realized I have no hood and no umbrella. I looked up only to realize I wasn't in the park anymore. I was in the middle of an abandoned street.

"Wyatt," I tried to call out in the rain.

Am I hallucinating or...or am I finally having a vision?

"Wyatt!"

"Aries!"

I quickly ran to the sound of his voice in the alleyway.

"Wyatt, where are you?!"

There was only silence. But over the rain, I heard grunting and something hitting flesh over and over. I ran over to the sound and saw a hooded figure smashing a hammer down onto Wyatt's head. No. NO! I fell to the ground as the hooded figure's sleeve came down revealing their tattoo. The gang member's tattoo.

"NO," I screamed over the rain.

Suddenly, the figure stopped. Did-Did he hear me? He slowly turned around and my heart sunk to the ground. I'm going to throw up. It was him? How could it be him? How could he betray us? After everything, we've been through.

As the rain poured down on us. Tears of anger and betrayal ran down my face as they stood in front of me. I looked up at them in rage. They stared at me and I stared right back into the eyes of Calum.

Chapter 19

He was covered in Wyatt's blood. Why? Why would he kill his own nephew? Suddenly, he smiled, sending a chill down my spine. He raised the hammer and I closed my eyes waiting for the impact.

"Aries?"

I opened my eyes and saw Wyatt in front of me.

"You okay?"

I looked at my hands shaking. Then, a drop of blood was on them. Then another. I felt underneath my nose and it was bleeding nonstop. I groaned in pain as a ringing surrounded my head. I covered my ears and it was wet. I pulled back my hands to find blood. I tried to speak but only blood came out. Wyatt was speaking but it was muffled. The ringing got louder and louder until I passed out.

I woke up to a bright light. I sat up and looked around. I was in a hospital room.

"Wyatt?"

I tried to get up but I was hooked up to an IV. Then, I heard gunshots and Wyatt yelling. I quickly pulled out the IVs and ran out into the hallway. It was empty and the lights were off except for one down the hallway. A girl was standing under it staring at me. She turned and walked away. I quickly followed her and she led me to Wyatt's body. He had a gunshot wound in his forehead. I backed away while hyperventilating. I was going to walk away but the girl grabbed my wrist with her icy fingers.

"You can't save him! Stop trying to save him!"

I woke up gasping for air.

"Hey, you're okay. You're in the hospital," Wyatt said.

No. No.

"I'll go get the doctor-."

"NO!"

"What? Why?"

"We gotta get out of here."

"Aries calm down."

"No, we have to leave!"

I ripped out the IV and Wyatt grabbed my wrist.

"Woah! Stop! What are you doing?!"

"It's Calum. It's been Calum this whole time and now we have to leave before he gets here!"

"He's already here."

My heart dropped.

"What?"

"Yeah, he's right outside."

Chapter 20

"Maybe you should get some re-."

I stood up while stumbling. Wyatt rushed to my side as I made my way to the window.

"What are you doing?"

I opened the window without answering him. I looked out to see a ledge and we were ten stories up. I looked to where the ledge ended and it led to a fire escape.

"Alright, if we shimmy our way to that fire escape we can get to the car or the bus or whatever."

"Aries, first of all, I'm not an acrobat, I'll most likely fall on my face. Second of all, you're too weak to move anywhere."

I quickly turned around and placed my hands on Wyatt's shoulders.

"CALUM MURDERED YOU! Don't you get it?"

"Calum wouldn't-."

"I thought that too but I saw him, Wyatt. He was smashing your head with a hammer and was going to do the same to me."

"When did you see that?"

"When I went to tie my shoe."

"I thought you said that nobody could see you in your visions."

"I-. Yeah but for some reason he did."

"Are you sure you weren't hallucinating? You haven't slept in days."

"Um-. I-. Um-."

What if it was a hallucination?

"Lie down and we'll wait for the doctor to come back in, okay?"

I nodded and laid on the bed. He laid next to me.

"I can't sleep."

"Do you want me to hum you a lullaby?"

"What am I? Five?"

He chuckled, making me smile.

"But, can you sing the incantation from *Tangled*?"

"I thought you said you weren't five?"

"It calms me."

He smiled and wrapped his arms around me while running his fingers through my hair. He sang softly in my ear. Maybe it was a hallucination. Calum loves Wyatt and paid for our wedding. Why would he kill someone he loves?

"Save what has been lost. Bring back what once was mine."

What once was mine," I whispered as I fell asleep.

Chapter 21

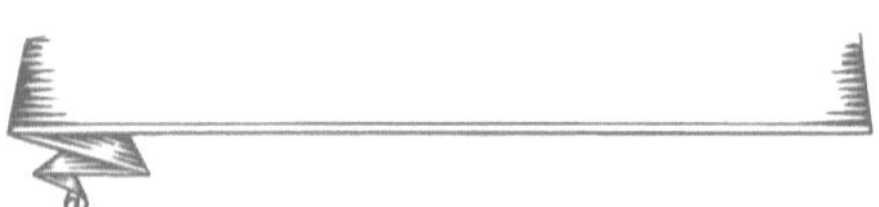

I woke up a few hours later. Wyatt was asleep next to me. I checked my phone and it was two in the morning. I was about to turn my phone off until I saw a message from Hayden.

Hay Hay

Hey, I'll be there in ten minutes

*Sent at 9:33 pm

That's weird. Why isn't he here? I sat up and texted him back.

Hey, where r u?

It's been way past ten minutes

Hay Hay is typing...

Sorry, I decided to just stay home. I'll visit you in the morning

I tapped my fingers on the back of my phone. I would've just left the conversation right there but I couldn't shake this anxious feeling in my chest.

Aight, good night then

By the way, how's ur pet hamster, Randy?

He's doing just fine

Good night

*Read at 2:05 am

I quickly shook Wyatt awake.

"Five more minutes."

"Wyatt, wake up, something's wrong."

"What do you mean," he asked while rubbing his eyes.

"I texted Hayden about his pet hamster, Randy and he said that he's doing fine."

Wyatt glared at me.

"You woke me up for that?"

"No Wyatt. Randy died eight years ago. We had a funeral for him and everything."

Wyatt sat up, fully awake now.

"What are you saying?"

"Hayden said at 9:33 that he would be here in ten minutes but he's still not here."

"Did you try calling him?"

I shook my head and called Hayden. We waited and waited. Hayden, please pick up. Then, I heard Hayden's ringtone but it was close. I took the IV out of my arm and got up.

"Aries?"

I called Hayden again and I heard his ringtone as I got closer to the door. I opened it and it was closer now. I felt Wyatt grab the bottom of my shirt as I went toward the ringtone. It stopped and I called Hayden again as my heart began pounding. The ringtone was blaring now as we stood in front of the janitor's closet. I put my hands on the knob shaking while the ringtone blared in my ear. I opened the door and there was nothing inside as the ringtone stopped. It was pitch black and there was a terrible smell. Wyatt said something but it was muffled. I called Hayden again and I screamed as his phone turned on in the darkness revealing Hayden's corpse.

As far as I could see, his neck was slit open and there was dried blood on his phone. I backed away, covering my mouth as I sobbed. The ringtone stopped and it was dark in the closet again as Wyatt shut the door. Wyatt knelt in front of me.

"Ari, I'm so sorry. But if someone was texting off his phone that means they're still-."

My phone ringing cut him off. I looked down and it was Hayden making my breathing pick up. I hesitantly answered.

"Hello?"

"I would start running if I were you."

That's when the closet door opened again.

Chapter 22

It was like everything was in slow motion. Wyatt grabbed my hand as soon as we heard the creaking of the closet door. He pulled me up and we started running back to my room as we heard footsteps coming toward us. Wyatt pushed me into the room first and he slammed the door closed behind us. He held the door closed as the person kept slamming against it.

"Aries, find something!"

I looked around and the only thing big enough to block the door was the bed. I quickly unplugged it and pushed it towards the door. Wyatt got out of the way as I blocked it.

"That won't hold. Remember your plan from earlier, we're going to have to do it."

He went to the window and opened it.

"Who's going first," I asked.

Wyatt silently cursed as he looked back between the door, the ledge, and me.

"You gotta go first," I said before he could.

"Aries-."

"Wyatt, go!"

He sighed and went out the window. He went alongside the ledge and I got out as the door burst open. I closed the window and grabbed the pipe next to it as the guy smashed the window open.

"Aries-."

"I'm right behind you, go!"

We shimmied across the ledge and finally made it to the fire escape. Wyatt climbed over and he helped me over the bar. We ran down the fire escape and were on the third floor when Wyatt suddenly stopped making me run into his back.

"What?"

"This is where it ends."

I looked ahead and he was right. They were still building it.

"Let's call the police while we still can."

"My phone is still in the room, do you still have yours?"

I checked my pockets and it wasn't there.

"I must've dropped it while we were running."

"Alright, we just have to make it to my car and get help. We can do that."

I started to nod but then I remembered my nightmare.

"Wyatt-."

He opened the window.

"Come on."

He crawled through and I quickly followed him. I have to keep Wyatt safe.

"Where are all the doctors and nurses, shouldn't someone have the night shift?"

"Wyatt-."

"Let's get to the elevator."

We ran around the corner to the elevator only for it to be out of order.

"Stairs!"

We ran down the stairs but then I started feeling dizzy. I stopped and closed my eyes. I felt Wyatt wrap my arms around his neck as he lifted me up. He ran down the stairs with me on his back. He suddenly stopped when we got to the bottom of the stairs.

"What's wrong," I asked weakly.

He let me off his back and gently set me on the stairs. He opened the door a bit to peek and he slowly closed it.

"My uncle is out there."

"Great, he can help us."

He looked at me with wide eyes.

"Aries, maybe your hallucination was a vision."

"What do you mean?"

"Think about it. People go through you and can't see you because you're not there when it happens. But when Calum saw you, you had to be there."

He's right.

"So you're saying-."

"I'm saying that...that you're right."

"I'm sorry, Wyatt."

"No, I'm sorry, I should've believed you and we would've been out of here by now."

"He's your uncle, of course, you wouldn't believe me."

"Well, he's after me so I'll distract him while you make a run for the car," he said handing me the keys.

I held his hand and smiled.

"I love you."

His eyes widened.

"Ari-."

I pulled him away from the door and threw him to the floor. I quickly opened the door, slid through, and closed it. I felt him pounding against it while yelling my name.

"Well hello, Aries. You're not the person I wanted to see."

"Why are you doing this?"

He sighed and started pacing.

"There's always a why in your little fairy tale, isn't there? Well, to give you your why, I'll just say, he killed my sister."

He scoffed.

"What an irony, both our sisters are dead."

"You're the boss. Why did you kill my sister?"

"I don't think you'll like the reason."

I glared at him.

"Alright, well that night I was doing the usual job. The client tried to attack me and of course, I killed them. It was supposed to be a normal night. But when I turn around, I see your sister staring at me. She saw me kill him and she had seen my face. I couldn't let her go so I had to kill her. Of course, she ran but obviously, I was faster. I slit her throat and drove her to the pier. I dumped her body into the lake and drove. Night done, one small mistake cleared up. Who knew that her brother would be marrying my nephew."

I clenched my fists in anger.

"And what about Wyatt?"

"Wyatt, well he was stealing from us and all I wanted was to fire him. But then, my sister's house caught on fire, and...well you know the rest. But what I didn't know was that one of my own had burned it down. I didn't find out until years later. I only kept Marco alive because I thought he could bring Wyatt to me so I could kill him myself. But I also had a backup plan. Mitchell. I told Mitchell that he could come back if he just did one simple job for me. To kill Wyatt and he was ecstatic about it. But then you got in the way and made everything so much more complicated."

"Why did you help us get married then?"

He shrugged.

"I just love weddings," he said laughing.

Then, he stopped and pulled out a gun.

"Now, move away from the door."

"Over my dead body."

He smirked.

"Okay."

He raised the gun and I moved in time as he shot at me. I ran behind the counter as he shot at me. I peeked over the counter and saw him going towards the door. I grabbed the vase on the counter and threw it. It hit his head, making him drop the gun. I charged at him and tackled him to the floor.

"Wyatt, go now!"

Calum threw me off him and got on top of me. He wrapped his hands around my neck and I felt around for something.

"You're just a mistake like your sister."

I felt one of the pieces of the vase and stabbed him in the eye making him scream in agony. I saw the gun and tried to grab it but he grabbed my foot and dragged me back. Then, he pulled out a knife and stabbed me in the leg making me scream in pain. He ran to the gun and grabbed it. He kicked open the door and I waited for him to shoot but it never came. Maybe Wyatt got out? Calum turned towards me and then Wyatt landed on him, making the gun slide towards me. I grabbed it as Calum threw Wyatt off him. He got out his knife and I pointed the gun at him. He went to stab him but I pulled the trigger and the shot echoed through the building. He held his chest as he fell to the ground. I ran to Wyatt and helped him up while dropping the gun.

"I told you to run."

"And I told you that I won't let you die like you, how you won't let me die."

I sighed as he held my hands.

"In sickness and health."

"Until death do us part," I finished.

We kissed and hugged. Then, I felt Wyatt go tense in my arms.

"Wyatt-."

"I love you."

He turned us around as a gunshot went off. I saw Calum drop the gun as he took his final breath. No. I looked down and saw Wyatt's body in my arms with a gunshot wound in his forehead. NO! I dropped to the floor along with Wyatt's body.

"You can't cheat death, Aries."

"You can't save him!"

All I could do was scream. Scream in rage. Scream in frustration. Scream because I lost him.

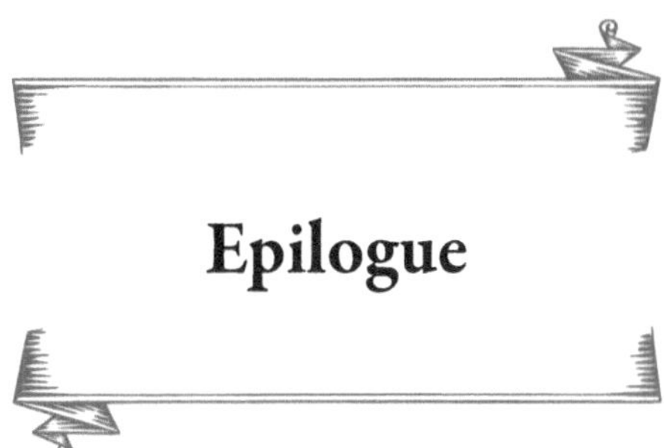

Epilogue

I can see my own future sometimes. It happens out of nowhere. I could be sitting in class or just lying in my bed. Obviously, since it's my future I can prevent it. But, after everything, I can't. I thought I could get my happily ever after but I can't.

My future was that I would go to the tallest building in Seattle, go to the ledge, and jump off. When I was younger, I always wondered why I would do that. I was always so scared that it would happen. But now, I'm not scared anymore.

I looked at my wedding ring and smiled. I turned my back to the ledge and leaned back, making me fall. Maybe I can't prevent the future after all.

The End

Don't miss out!

Visit the website below and you can sign up to receive emails whenever DeJane Penick publishes a new book. There's no charge and no obligation.

https://books2read.com/r/B-A-MVJR-EVIAC

BOOKS 2 READ

Connecting independent readers to independent writers.

Did you love *If Happy Ever Afters Did Exist*? Then you should read *Say You'll Remember Me*[1] by DeJane Penick!

[2]

Michael has been able to see ghosts since he was five. Nobody including his parents believe him and his mother ends up sending him to a mental institution. After he gets out at 18, he gets an apartment of his own and tries his best to ignore his ability.

Four years later, Michael now is in Law school and has a beautiful girlfriend named Chloe and hasn't seen a single ghost. Until Chloe's ex-boyfriend, Paris dies from a drug overdose in South Korea. His ghost tries to convince Michael that his death was a murder and that Michael can help him solve it. Michael eventually gives in only to get rid of him but he didn't expect to fall in love with him or that Paris's murderer will stop at nothing to keep Paris's death buried.

---

1. https://books2read.com/u/3JEaqP

2. https://books2read.com/u/3JEaqP